D1420755

For baby Teddy Aldrich, with lots of love
~ M C B

For Mormor, Margrethe Kristensen
~ T M

LITTLE TIGER PRESS
An imprint of Magi Publications
1 The Coda Centre, 189 Munster Road,
London SW6 6AW
www.littletigerpress.com

First published in Great Britain 2005

A CIP catalogue record for this book is
available from the British Library

Printed in China

10 9 8 7 6 5 4 3 2

Snow Friends

M Christina Butler
Tina Macnaughton

LITTLE TIGER PRESS
London

Little Bear woke early from his deep winter sleep.
As he yawned and stretched he looked out of the
bear cave and gasped. The world was covered with
a thick white blanket, sparkling in the sunshine!
"Oooh!" he cried, "snow!" and he raced out to play.

Little Bear went rolling and skidding down the hillside, racing faster and faster.

He rushed through the trees, shaking the branches to make tiny white snow storms. He stomped and stamped in the crunchy snow, making trails of footprints that circled and twirled.

Little Bear climbed up a hill and gazed out at the whiteness. The mountains and forests were still and silent. He looked around for someone to play with, but he couldn't see anyone . . . anywhere.

"Hellooo!" he cried. "Hellooo!" came back his echo. But no one else replied. Little Bear was all alone.

"Oh dear," he sighed. "If only
I had someone to play with."
And he fell with a plop into
a big snowdrift.

Suddenly Little Bear had an idea. He began
to make a snowball, bigger and bigger.
"If I make a *really* big snowball," he thought,
"I could build a snowman, and *then* I would
have someone to play with!"
So he rolled and rolled a shiny round
snowman body until it was nearly as big
as he was!

Little Bear was so busy with his snowball that he didn't see Otter swimming across the lake.

"Hello!" cried Otter, racing up. "What are you doing?"

"I'm making a snowman. The best snowman EVER!" replied Little Bear.

"Wow!" said Otter. "That sounds fun. Can I help?"

"That would be great," said Little Bear.
And they pushed and they puffed
until they couldn't roll the snowball
any further.

Little Bear and Otter stopped for a rest, but just then they heard a muffled voice.

"Hey! What's going on?" it cried. "Everything's gone dark!"

"My snowball's talking!" squeaked Little Bear.

"No," laughed Otter. "The noise is underneath. Quick!" And together they pushed as hard as they could until the big snowball creaked away to one side.

A rabbit popped up from his burrow.
"Who turned off the light!" he said crossly.

"Sorry," said Little Bear. "We're building the best snowman EVER!"

"And it got stuck on top of your burrow," giggled Otter.

"Funny snowman," said Rabbit, laughing. "It hasn't got a head!"

"We haven't made his head yet," said Little Bear. "You can help if you like."

So Rabbit helped to make
the snowman's head, and
gave him a big happy smile.

Then Otter went back
    to the river for some sticks, and
        Little Bear found a few nuts left in his winter
            store, while Rabbit picked out the very best
                carrot from his larder . . .

They built the snowman together, with Otter's sticks for arms, and the nuts from Little Bear's store for his eyes. Finally Rabbit climbed on to Little Bear's shoulders and pushed the carrot nose in place.

Otter laughed and cheered, "Hooray!"

The BEST SNOWMAN EVER was finished!

For the rest of the day they played
with the snowman in the snow. They
played hide and seek and chase, and
had huge snowball fights that left
them giggling and gasping for breath.

At last, as the sky turned orange and the sun set, the three friends talked about what games they would play the next day.

"Let's go exploring," said Rabbit.

"But what about Snowman?" said Little Bear. "We can't leave him all on his own."

"Let's build him a friend, then!" said Otter.

Once again they rolled and patted and
shaped, until they made a perfect little
snowman.

By the time they had finished the stars were twinkling in the sky. Tired and happy they crashed in a heap and watched with wonder as the snowman and his friend turned to silver in the moonlight.

"He's the BESTEST SNOWMAN IN THE WORLD," whispered Little Bear.

"And he'll never be lonely now he has a friend," said Otter.

"Yes," Rabbit smiled. "Just like us!"